Horses' Night Out

A SIROCCO STORY

By Sibley Miller

Illustrated by Tara Larsen Chang and Jo Gershman

Feiwel and Friends

For Brian, Adam, Brett, and Seth—Sibley Miller

For Norman, for enthusiastic, educated, manly input
—Tara Larsen Chang

For Danny, who patiently listens to all of my horse tales
—Jo Gershman

A FEIWEL AND FRIENDS BOOK
An Imprint of Macmillan

WIND DANCERS: HORSES' NIGHT OUT Copyright © 2008
by Reeves International, Inc. All rights reserved. BREYER,
WIND DANCERS, and BREYER logos are trademarks and/or registered
trademarks of Reeves International, Inc. Printed in China.
For information, address Feiwel and Friends,
175 Fifth Avenue, New York, N.Y. 10010.

Library of Congress Cataloging-in-Publication Data

Miller, Sibley.
Horses' night out : a Sirocco story / by Sibley Miller.
p. cm. — (Wind Dancers ; #4)
Summary: When Sirocco leads the tiny, winged fillies on a night-time
adventure, he discovers that he is afraid of the dark, as well as that
their human friend, Leanna, needs a "sleep buddy."
ISBN-13: 978-0-312-38283-4 / ISBN-10: 0-312-38283-9
[1. Magic—Fiction. 2. Horses—Fiction. 3. Night—Fiction. 4. Fear of
the dark—Fiction.] I. Title.   PZ7.M63373Hov 2008   [E]—dc22
2008012789

DESIGNED BY BARBARA GRZESLO
Feiwel and Friends logo designed by Filomena Tuosto

First Edition: November 2008

1   3   5   7   9   10   8   6   4   2

www.feiwelandfriends.com

CONTENTS

Meet the Wind Dancers

One day, a lonely little girl named Leanna blows on a doozy of a dandelion. To her delight and surprise, four tiny horses spring from the puff of the dandelion seeds!

Four tiny horses with shiny manes and shimmery wings. Four magical horses who can fly!

Dancing on the wind, surrounded by magic halos, they are the Wind Dancers.

The leader of the quartet is **Kona**. She has a violet-black coat and vivid purple mane, and she flies inside a halo of magical flowers.

Brisa is as pretty as a tropical sunset with her coral-pink color and blond mane and tail.

Magical jewels make up Brisa's halo, and she likes to admire her gems (and herself) every time she looks in a mirror.

Sumatra is silvery blue with sea-green wings. Much like the ocean, she can shift from calm to stormy in a hurry! Her magical halo is made up of ribbons, which flutter and dance as she flies.

The fourth Wind Dancer is—surprise!—a colt. His name is Sirocco. He's a fiery gold, and he likes to go-go-go. Everywhere he goes, his magical halo of butterflies goes, too.

The tiny, flying horses live together in the dandelion meadow in a lovely house carved out of the trunk of an apple tree. Every day, Leanna wishes she'll see the magical little horses again. (She's sure they're nearby, but she doesn't know they're invisible to people.) And, the Wind Dancers get ready for their next adventure.

CHAPTER 1

Rise and . . . Shine?

In the sleeping stalls of the Wind Dancers' apple tree house, all was quiet.

Well, sort of quiet.

Kona was snoring noisily from beneath her horse blanket.

Brisa was giggling her way through a funny dream.

Sumatra's feet were *tap, tap, tapping* on her stall's wooden floor as she dreamed she was dancing in the air.

And Sirocco's stomach was growling. *Loudly.*

"Mmmm," Sirocco murmured in his sleep, his closed eyes smiling. "A second helping of shoofly pie? Don't mind if I do. I hate flies, but I love pie!"

As Sirocco bit into the pie in his dream, his *actual* teeth began *click, clack, clicking*.

His lips smacked wetly.

And he swallowed dramatically with great, big *galumphs*, even though all he was really swallowing was air.

"Yum!" said the sleeping horse.

Of course, in real life, Sirocco's belly was still empty. His stomach was *so* noisy, in fact, that it woke him up!

As Sirocco's eyes blinked open, he smacked his lips again. Then he sighed.

Too bad, he thought to himself. *I can't taste that shoofly pie at all. I guess I was dreaming, for sure.*

In the glow of his night-light—actually, a

 8

few friendly fireflies—Sirocco looked over at his sleep buddy, a fuzzy green and orange stuffed frog named Jeepers. The cute little toy was plunked on top of his stall wall.

"Well, Jeepers," Sirocco said, "if I can't have dream pie, I might as well get me some *real* breakfast. I wonder what Kona's making this morning!"

Sirocco was so eager to start a new day—and to start it with *food*—that he reared back in his stall with a happy whinny. His kicking front hoof caught Jeepers and tossed him into the air. The frog did a quick double flip before landing on the floor with a plop!

"*Ha, ha, ha!*" Sirocco laughed at Jeepers' gymnastic move. Then he trotted out of his stall.

"See you later, Jeepers," he called over his shoulder.

His stomach still growling loudly, Sirocco galloped upstairs to the kitchen.

"Good morrrrning," he neighed as he approached the kitchen door. "What's for breakfa—"

Sirocco skidded to a stop. The kitchen was empty! Well, except for even more fireflies, which were circling the ceiling and giving off a pretty yellow light. No horses were pouring oats into feed buckets or mashing apples into applesauce or drawing nice, cold rainwater into the water trough. And there was, *for sure*, no shoofly pie.

"Well," Sirocco said to himself, "I can do something about *that*!"

He turned around and *clop, clop, clopped*

down to his friends' sleeping stalls, yelling, "Wake up, sleepyheads! Time for breakfast!"

Sirocco whinnied into Brisa's stall first, then Kona's, and finally Sumatra's—until all three fillies reluctantly woke up. Shaking their heads sleepily, they dragged themselves out of their cozy stalls and loped up to the kitchen.

Dangling from Brisa's teeth was her sleep buddy, a tiny horse with a comb-able mane and tail named Brisina. 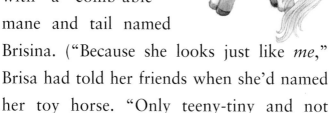 ("Because she looks just like *me*," Brisa had told her friends when she'd named her toy horse. "Only teeny-tiny and not *quite* as pretty.")

Kona's teddy bear— whom she'd given the nice, sensible name Charles—was perched on her neck like a little jockey.

And Sumatra's small security blanket—
which she'd woven with her satiny magic ribbons—
was draped over her back.

"Siroooocccco," Brisa complained, shaking her tousled, blond forelock out of her eyes. "Why did you drag Brisina and me away from our beauty sleep?"

"For breakfast, of course!" Sirocco said.

"I'm too tired to eat," Sumatra said through a giant yawn. Her green eyelashes drooped and her tail hung listlessly.

"And *I'm* too tired to *make* anything to eat," Kona said. All the flowers in her magic halo were tightly closed. They were still sleepy, too.

Sirocco stared at the fillies in disgust.

"What do you mean *tired*?" he demanded.

"You've been sleeping all night! The day's going to get away from us!"

Sumatra gazed out the kitchen window for a moment. Then she frowned and turned to the colt.

"Sirocco," she said sternly, "there *is* no day!"

"What do you mean?" Sirocco said. "We're awake, aren't we? So it *must* be day."

Sumatra looked out the window again and used her nose to point through it.

"Look," she said wearily.

Sirocco trotted over and peered out the window.

"Look at what?" he said impatiently. "I can't see anything."

"Exactly," Kona said, joining Sumatra and Sirocco by the window. "You can't see anything because it's dark out. It's still nighttime!"

"You woke up early, Sirocco," Brisa said with a sleepy shrug. "Let's go back to bed."

"*Aw,*" Sirocco complained. "I can't go back to bed now. I'm *awake*. And so are all of you. Who cares if it's daytime or night-time? We should go *do* something."

Sumatra stopped yawning and stretching and stared at the colt.

"Sirocco," she scolded, "horses stay awake during the day and we sleep at night. It's the way things are! You can't just go *switching things around*!"

"Why not?!" Sirocco challenged her with an impish grin.

"Here's why!" Brisa piped up. She placed Brisina on the kitchen table and anxiously stroked the toy horse's mane with her nose. "We've never been out at night. It might be scary out there."

"Please," Sirocco said, waving his hoof at

Brisa. "I've heard there are lots of animals who stay up all night—owls and bats and raccoons. If it was so scary at night, they'd stay home!"

"But we don't *know* those owls and bats and raccoons," Sumatra pointed out. "That means they're *strangers*. And you know what they say . . ."

"No, what?" Sirocco asked.

"Stranger danger!" Sumatra replied, looking frightened.

Sirocco's eyes went wide. His mouth began to tremble.

"When you put it that way . . ." he began.

The fillies glanced at each other hopefully. Maybe they'd finally persuaded Sirocco to let them go back to bed!

". . . that makes me want to go out more than ever!" Sirocco finished with an excited whinny.

"Okay, so he's *not* scared," Kona muttered to Sumatra and Brisa.

Sirocco tapped his hooves impatiently and shot longing looks at the window.

"You know Sirocco," Sumatra whispered to the other fillies. "When he's *this* excited, there's no stopping him."

"And it *will* be hard to get back to sleep after all our chitchat," Brisa whispered back. The jewels in her magic halo had brightened. They looked almost as ready for adventure as Sirocco was.

Kona shrugged.

"Okay!" she announced to Sirocco. "I guess we're going out!"

"Yeah!" Sirocco cried. "Hey, before we

go, can someone make me some shoofly pie for breakfast? It was so yummy in my dream."

Sumatra gaped at Sirocco.

"Don't push your luck, night owl!" she blurted.

Sirocco laughed.

"Hey," he defended himself, "you can't blame me for trying!"

The fillies laughed, too, as they threw together a much-easier-than-shoofly-pie breakfast: some apples, oats, and carrots. Then—chattering excitedly—they tromped up to the tree house's top floor and gathered at the front door.

As the horses got ready to take flight, Sumatra used her teeth to tie her ribbon-y security blanket around her neck.

Kona twisted her head around and tucked her teddy bear tightly under her flower necklace so he wouldn't fall off while she flew.

And Brisa used her teeth to hook Brisina's sparkly reins over one of the jewels in her magic halo.

"Why are you all bringing your sleep buddies?" Sirocco asked with a teasing grin. "You're not scared of the dark, are you?"

"No!" Kona said defensively. She turned around and gave Charles a protective nuzzle with her silky soft nose. "It's just . . . you never know when you're going to need your teddy bear, that's all."

Sumatra and Brisa nodded emphatically.

"We're not scared," Sumatra agreed, snuggling her blanket. "We're *prepared*."

"Don't you want to bring Jeepers?" Brisa asked Sirocco.

"Nope! Why would I do that?" Sirocco scoffed, waving his hoof at Brisa. "Let's go already," he urged the fillies. "It's time for a little night adventure!"

CHAPTER 2

Ghost Story

As Sirocco and the fillies flew into the night sky, they gasped.

"Everything is so different than it is in the daytime!" Kona said.

At least, Sirocco was pretty *sure* it was Kona who'd said this. In the dark night air, lit only by silvery moonlight, the violet-black filly was hard to see! Sirocco could *just* make out her snowy white forelegs as she flew.

Other night-time things felt odd to Sirocco, too.

The full moon floated eerily in the sky.

Sirocco felt like it was staring down at him! And the stars were so distant, they made Sirocco feel even tinier than he already was.

The dandelion meadow felt huge, too. During the day, Sirocco could see the entire field, from Leanna's tidy farmhouse to the horse paddock to the forest. Now, Leanna's yellow house had been reduced to the faint glow of the front-porch light. Sirocco couldn't even *see* the paddock. And the forest was a dark blot on the horizon.

While Sirocco tried (a little desperately) to get his bearings, Sumatra sighed happily.

"I think this must be what it's like to swim in the ocean," she said, gliding lazily on an air current. "You're just floating around in a whole lot of nothing."

"Ooh, you're so right," Brisa agreed pleasantly.

Yeah, you are *right,* Sirocco thought—not so pleasantly.

"You know the strangest thing about being out at night?" Kona said. "It doesn't feel scary! In fact, I kind of like it out here!"

You do?! Sirocco thought as he warily eyed the giant moon.

"I *know*!" Sumatra replied in surprise. "I feel the same way. Sure, the air's a little chilly, but my buddy blanket is keeping me warm."

Sirocco, who didn't have a blanket or a buddy, just shivered.

"The only thing I *don't* like about the night," Brisa noted, "is that nobody can see how pretty I am in the dark."

"Oh, that's not true," Kona said kindly. "Your pink coat gives off a beautiful glow in the moonlight."

"Really?" Brisa cooed. "Well, then I *love* night! And so does Brisina."

It was Sirocco's turn to say how fabulous the dark was. The only problem was—Sirocco couldn't think of *anything* fabulous to say!

"Uh, Sirocco?" Kona asked. "Are you having fun on our night out?"

Sirocco jumped.

"Of course, I'm having fun!" he brayed.

Or rather, he *tried* to bray. But the sound that came out was more of a . . . squeak.

A *frightened* squeak.

But that's impossible! Sirocco thought to himself with a frown. *I'm not scared. I can't be scared. I don't do scared.*

And just to prove the point to himself—or to any other Wind Dancer who might be watching—Sirocco did a loop-de-loop in the

cool, damp night air.

"Ha, ha!" he laughed. This time, his voice sounded a bit stronger.

See! he told himself triumphantly. *I'm not scared at all—*

Suddenly, Sirocco's thought froze in his mind. His body went cold, as well. And his wings began to flap in panic.

He'd seen something!

Something skimming silently along the grass beneath him.

It was black.

And swift.

And it pulsated madly, like a beating heart!

Sirocco pointed a trembling hoof at the ground.

"There's a g-g-gho—" he stammered to his friends.

"What, Sirocco?" Brisa asked breezily, as she swooped around in the dark.

"Look down," Sirocco gasped, his little horse knees practically knocking together. "It's a g-g-gho—"

"Wow, look at that!"

That was Kona. And *she* was pointing down at the gliding ghost! But instead of being terrified, she was smiling!

Sirocco wasn't sure what was going on. And he would definitely have said so if he wasn't scared speechless by the ghost—*which was still directly underneath him!*

Inexplicably, Kona chattered on.

"Sirocco's shadow looks so neat in the light of the moon," she said. "It almost looks like a ghost!"

"*Eeek!* I'm scared!" Brisa joked, while Sumatra laughed along. The two of them began giggling and swooping around in the air, hooting like ghosts.

Sirocco looked again at his "ghost." He waved one hoof at it. It waved back at him! Sirocco's mouth dropped open.

My 'ghost,' he thought to himself, *was nothing more than my shadow?!*

Sirocco snuck a glance at the fillies. They were still playing.

Whew! Sirocco thought in relief. His friends had been so busy having fun, they hadn't noticed his fear.

Then he looked again at his shadow, which now seemed perfectly harmless.

You know, he mused in his head, *maybe I was a little scared when I thought my shadow was a ghost. But mostly I was . . . just getting ready for action.*

And—as Sirocco joined his friends, swooping and hooting himself—he almost believed his own story!

. . .

"What should we do now?" Sirocco asked exuberantly after the Wind Dancers had almost worn themselves out flying in the night air. All memories of his fright had by then melted away.

"Well," Kona said thoughtfully, "shadows are so different at night. Let's go see what *else* is different when it's dark out."

"Ooh, let's!" Brisa agreed.

"We'll go to the woods," Kona declared. She flapped her wings eagerly. Charles the teddy bear, who was still perched on her neck, seemed to nod.

But Sirocco felt himself get a little shivery.

"The woods?" he asked. "Um, I thought you preferred Leanna's farmhouse, Kona. You know, the one with the *lights*."

"Isn't the whole point of this adventure to be out in the *dark*?" Sumatra pointed out. "You're not scared, are you?"

"What?" Sirocco said quickly. He felt his face go hot. "No! Of course I'm not scared. No way! Not me! Not even a little bi—"

"Okay, okay," Sumatra interrupted with a laugh. "You've made your point, Sirocco."

Triumphant, Sirocco grinned at the fillies.

"Okay, so we'll go to the woods," he said brashly. "In fact, I say we *race*. I'm sure I'll win. *You* guys are going to be slowed down by your teddy bear and blanket and toy horse."

Brisa turned toward Brisina, who was still dangling from a jewel in her halo. She gave the doll a sweet nuzzle with her nose.

"Don't listen to him, Brisina," Brisa said loudly. "Sirocco's just saying that because *he* misses Jeepers."

"Do not!" Sirocco said with a grin. And before he had a chance to imagine Jeepers' comforting fuzzy face, he pawed the air with his hoof.

"Last one to the woods is a rotten apple!" he declared. "OnyourmarkgetsetGO!"

He zipped toward the forest.

"Hey!" Sumatra neighed after him. "No fair getting a head start!"

"Well, you better get moving then," Sirocco yelled over his shoulder with a laugh.

The three fillies flapped their wings and began flying after him.

Still laughing, Sirocco flew with all his might. Racing with his friends was just like their usual daytime fun! Sirocco almost forgot that they were doing it at night, surrounded by black sky instead of blue.

That is, he almost forgot until he dove into the forest!

The moment Sirocco ducked between the trees, the blackness got blacker.

The shadows got more shadowy.

And the chilly, clammy air got chillier and clammier!

But all that was nothing compared with the horrible sounds that met Sirocco's ears.

The noise was deafening!

CHAPTER 3

A Little Night Music

A moment after Sirocco arrived in the *horribly noisy* forest, Kona, Brisa, and Sumatra joined him.

"Wow!" Sumatra yelled excitedly. "What is all this racket?"

Sirocco spun around in the air, feeling dizzy and confused.

But not scared, he insisted to himself. *It's just a little noise, that's all. Just some whirring.*

And buzzing.

And chirping!

And HOOTING!

And there, off in the distance, did Sirocco detect a mean growl? He clenched his teeth to keep from whinnying in fright. Meanwhile, Kona spoke loudly over the noise.

"Listen to that!" she said with wonder. "In the daytime, the forest just sounds like rustling leaves."

"And a babbling creek," Sumatra agreed.

"And the chirping of cute little birds," Brisa added, looking around. "I wonder where all these *neat* noises are coming from."

"Yeah," Sirocco said nervously. "Neat noises! That's just what I was thinking."

Hoo-hoo-HOOT!

"Ooh," Sumatra cried. "I think I know where *that* sound came from! Look!"

She pointed with her nose up into the dark shadows of the treetops. At first, Sirocco didn't see anything. Then, he spotted a flutter

of gray-brown feathers that were *swoop, swoop, swooping* through the air.

It was an owl! An owl with a sharp, curved beak! And giant, yellow, unblinking eyes! And that loud, horrible—

HOOT!

"*Aaaah!*" Sirocco cried.

"I *know!*" Sumatra said, looking at

Sirocco with gleaming eyes. "It *is* an amazing sound, isn't it?"

Sirocco blinked at her.

"Amazing?!" Sirocco sputtered. "More like terrify—"

But before he could finish his sentence, he noticed that Kona and Brisa were looking at him with the same bright eyes as Sumatra. *They* weren't terrified by the horrible hooting.

So, Sirocco decided, neither was he.

"Terri*fic*," he corrected himself quickly. "That's what I'd call that hoot! In fact, I bet I can hoot, too!"

Sirocco threw back his head.

 36

"*Hoo-hoo-hooooooot!*" he brayed.

The three fillies burst out laughing.

"That hoot sounds like a horse with a head cold to me," Sumatra said.

Trembling, Sirocco glanced back up into the treetops. Clearly, the owl didn't think any more of the colt's hoot than Sumatra did. The bird gave Sirocco a disdainful glare before turning feathery tail and flying deeper into the woods.

"Ha," Sirocco laughed weakly. But it was hard to pretend he was enjoying himself. He was too busy looking around for the *next* scary sound to come the Wind Dancers' way.

"Hey," he finally suggested to his friends, trying to sound chipper. "Why don't we go rest on a tree branch for a minute?"

Still giggling, the fillies agreed, and they followed Sirocco to a nearby branch. As soon as they rested, though, yet another new sound grew close.

But for once, it wasn't scary!

In fact, it was a pretty, lilting chirp.

And the horses only had to look around the tree where they were resting to see where the sound was coming from. Perched all over the tree's branches were lots of tiny crickets! The insects were rubbing their scratchy little wings together. With each scrape, the crickets made a sweet chirp.

"Now *there's* a sound I can really get behind!" Sirocco said to the fillies.

"Oh, please," Sumatra scoffed. "There's no way that your horsey voice can imitate a cricket's chirp."

"Who said I was going to use my voice?" Sirocco said, fluttering off of the tree branch with a laugh. Perhaps because the crickets' song was so pretty (or maybe because the crickets were so harmlessly small), Sirocco was feeling happy—and brave—for the first time since arriving in the woods.

He flew a few feet away from the tree branch, then turned to face the fillies.

"Chirping looks simple enough," he said, glancing again at the tree crickets sawing away with their wings. "You just rub your wings together, like so!"

Sirocco pressed his yellow-gold wings together and rubbed them up and down.

But instead of beautiful, chirpy music, his wings just made a soft, rustling sound. Sirocco was barely able to hear it over the din of the forest. He cocked his ears and listened harder.

He listened *so* hard, in fact, that he didn't realize something.

When he began vigorously rubbing his

wings together, he stopped *flapping* them. And that meant—

"Sirocco!" Sumatra neighed. "You're falling!"

But Sirocco couldn't see the ground through the pitch-black darkness. He had no idea how far away—or how close—he was to crashing to the forest floor!

CHAPTER 4

Star Light, Star Bright?

Neeeeeiggh—OOF!

Sirocco had landed.

But instead of crashing to the earth with a *splat*, he'd hit a body of water with a *splash*.

"Where am I?" Sirocco squeaked. He thrashed around in the water in fear.

"Have I broken my nose? What about my ears? Or my tail! I bet I've broken my tail!"

It took a few more moments of panicked splashing about for Sirocco to realize that he was actually—fine.

He was sitting in a mud puddle.

He was wet, shivering, and embarrassed.
But he was fine.

Until, of course, he wasn't. And *that* moment came when Sirocco felt something cold and *slimy* brush against his leg.

"*Aaaah!*" Sirocco neighed. "Don't tell me I survived that fall just to be swallowed up by a swamp creature!"

Suddenly, two bulgy eyes rose out of the puddle—and looked right at Sirocco! "*Peep, peep.*"

"What are you?" Sirocco shrieked. "Some sort of puddle monster?"

"I'm a peeper. A spring peeper, to be exact," said the bug-eyed creature.

The eyes rose further out of the water, revealing the slick head and body of a—

"Frog!" Sirocco cried. "You're a frog!"

"Yup," the peeper said. "*Peep, peep.*"

For the first time since the night-time

adventure had begun, Sirocco stopped feeling
shivery and shaky.

"I love frogs," he told Peeper. "I even have
a froggy sleep buddy. His name is Jeepers."

"I like the name," the frog said. "It rhymes
with peepers."

His bulgy eyes looked this way and that.
"So where *is* this Jeepers?"

Sirocco felt suddenly sad.

"At home," he murmured.

Just then, what seemed like a hundred pairs of bulgy eyes rose out of the puddle!

"*Peep, peep, peep!*" they croaked all together.

"Oh, wow!" Sirocco said, gazing at the froggy crowd. "Now I *really* miss Jeepers."

Suddenly, Kona's voice rang out from up above.

"Sirocco?" she called. "We can't see you down there. Are you okay?"

"I'm fine," Sirocco called up to his friends. His voice sounded thin and raspy. "I landed in a mud puddle."

Relieved, his filly friends answered with a chorus of laughs.

"What's wrong with me?" he whispered to his new peeper friend. "I'm on an adventure. But I'm not acting so adventurous!"

The frog shrugged.

"Don't ask me about adventure," he answered. "I never leave my puddle. My idea of a good time is a nice mud-mask facial and a mouthful of flies."

"Ooh," Sirocco said with a shudder. "I could never stay in one place my whole life. I was born to *fly*!"

"Oh, really," the frog said teasingly. "Seems to me you're a stick-in-the-mud like me. That's not exactly flying, is it?"

Sirocco stared at the frog. He felt his clenched mouth slowly widen into a grin.

"You know what?" Sirocco said. He stood up in the puddle and shook the mud off his wings. "You're right! It's time to stop moping and start *adventuring*!"

"Well, fly away, then," the peeper said.

"Have fun, *peep, peep*."

"Thanks, Mr. Peeper," Sirocco said. He puffed out his chest. Even if he didn't have the real Jeepers with him, the peeper had given him a burst of bravery!

Sirocco flew up to rejoin his friends. As he arrived back at the cricket tree, Brisa joyfully turned to the toy horse dangling from one of her magic jewels.

"See, Brisina," she said to the doll, "Sirocco's just fine."

Brisa looked at Sirocco with her beautiful big eyes.

"You had Brisina scared to death!" she said to the colt.

"Scared!" Sirocco scoffed. "That's silly!"

"I know, that's what I told her," Brisa said. "First, being scared gives you scrunched-up lines around the eyes, which are *not* pretty. Second, why should you be scared just because everything's so different at night?"

"Right!" Sirocco declared. "Anyway, I'm *not* scared." He tried to ignore the fact that his shivers had suddenly returned.

He was *so* shivery that he didn't see the fillies glance at each other.

"Well," Sumatra said carefully, "I'm glad you're not scared, Sirocco. After all, there's nothing scary about cool, damp night air."

"Right," Sirocco repeated. But now, his voice sounded weak again.

"And I like the strange shapes you see in the tree branches," Kona said happily.

"And don't forget the night music," Brisa added. "It's so tuneful."

Sirocco's heart was again beating fast. Any happiness he'd gotten from the Jeepers-like peepers had fizzled. He was quaking!

Is it because they all brought their sleep buddies that Brisa, Sumatra, and Kona are having such fun out here in the dark? he wondered. *Or is it because they're braver than me? Am I just one big scaredy-horse!?*

The thought made Sirocco shudder. He was a magical, flying colt. An adventurer. A Wind Dancer! The *last* thing he wanted to be was a scaredy-horse. Especially if the fillies weren't afraid.

Jeepers would be disappointed in me if he was here, Sirocco thought sadly. *Almost as disappointed as I am with myself.*

He hung his head—which was why he didn't see Kona, Sumatra, and Brisa exchange another quick glance.

"Hey, speaking of strange shapes,"

Sumatra said thoughtfully, "I miss the moon shadows of the meadow. What do you say we leave the forest and go back there?"

"Ooh, yes," Brisa agreed with a wink at Sumatra. "It's so nice and sparkly there, with the stars overhead and all."

"And the nice, *quiet* dandelions below," Kona added.

"And absolutely no ghosts," Sumatra added with a giggle.

Sirocco cocked his head.

"Okay, fillies, if you say so!" he said.

It was *such* a good idea that suddenly Sirocco felt much better.

"And you know what?" he added happily. "*I'll* lead the way!"

Sirocco reared back in the air, and began to fly as fast as he could toward the dandelion meadow. Kona, Sumatra, and Brisa followed with happy whinnies.

Before Sirocco knew it, they'd emerged from the trees and were skimming over the meadow they call home. The moon had risen higher in the sky, and it seemed brighter as well. So did the twinkling stars.

"*Aaaah!*" Sirocco sighed to himself. "Now *this* is more like it!"

In the moonlight, he grew more confident than ever. He could make out the grass beneath him (though it looked silver instead of green) and the Wind Dancers' apple tree (even if the branches looked creepy). Glancing over his shoulder at the fillies, Sirocco could even see black-as-night Kona.

Grinning hard, Sirocco faced forward again and flapped his wings powerfully, for the first time loving the feel of the cool night air rustling through his mane.

"So, what should we do now?" he called out to the horses behind him. "Maybe we should introduce ourselves to more night creatures."

"Hey, if you don't wait up," Sumatra called after Sirocco, "you'll be introducing yourself alone! Stop flying so fast!"

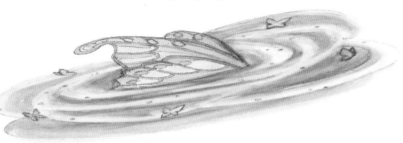

But Sirocco was thrilled not to be afraid anymore. And a happy Sirocco was a swift Sirocco. Without looking back, he yelled out, "Maybe you girls should *start* flying so fast. Try it, why don't y—huh? Wait a minute, what's happening?"

Sirocco blinked hard in confusion as he flew onward.

Because suddenly, he couldn't see!

Not a thing!

Sirocco looked up. The moon, which had been smiling down upon him a moment ago, had disappeared. The grass beneath him had gone from silver to black. The apple tree had disappeared from view altogether.

And worst of all, the sudden blackness had cut Sirocco off from his friends!

"Kona? Sumatra?" Sirocco called as he flew. "Brisa? Are you still behind me?"

There was no answer.

Only silence—and the sound of the wind whistling past Sirocco's ears. Sirocco fluttered to a stop and turned toward the fillies (or at least, he turned to where he *thought* the fillies ought to be).

"Hey, you guys!" he neighed. "Catch up, slowpokes."

He laughed as he teased his friends, but it was a nervous laugh.

And nobody giggled in response.

They were gone! Sirocco realized. He was all alone.

In the pitch-black night.

"Okay, that does it!" Sirocco whinnied. He felt his tail shoot up in the air. "I'm officially *scaaaaaared*!" he screamed.

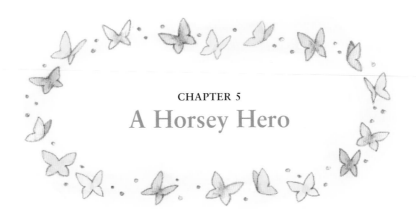

CHAPTER 5

A Horsey Hero

Brisa, Kona, and Sumatra hovered in the air, clustered closely together. They could feel the tips of their wings brush against each other.

"What just happened?" Brisa quavered.

"I think the moon hid behind a cloud," Sumatra said.

"No, I think the *cloud* floated in front of the *moon*," Kona corrected her.

"Oh, really, Miss Bossyhooves?" Sumatra replied. "Well, what do *you* think, Sirocco? Is this the moon's fault, or the cloud's?"

She waited for the colt to jump in.

"Where's Sirocco?" Sumatra neighed.

"He must have been too far ahead of us when the lights went out," Brisa said.

"Listen," Kona assured her friends. "Let's just stay put. When the moonlight comes back, Sirocco will find us easily."

"I guess that sounds like a good idea," Brisa said with a sigh. "But it's still not very fun, being stuck here in the dark."

"At least we have each other," Kona said. She reached her nose out into the darkness to touch Brisa's nose.

"Um, why are you poking at my flank with your nose?" Brisa asked politely.

"*Whoops*, sorry," Kona said with a giggle.

"It's hard to snuggle in the dark. Maybe we should just hang on to our sleep buddies."

"Ooh, I almost forgot Brisina was here!" Brisa said happily. Nosing around in the blackness, she found Brisina dangling off her magic jewel and plucked her up with her teeth. Immediately, she felt a little better.

Sumatra, too, reached around and pulled her ribbon-y blanket off her back. She held it between her teeth and stroked it with her foreleg.

And Kona twisted around to nuzzle her teddy bear, who was still propped on the back of her neck.

"Don't worry, Charles," she whispered to the fuzzy bear. "We'll be just fine until the lights come back."

. . .

Meanwhile, Sirocco couldn't have felt less fine. He flew and flew and *flew*—calling out his friends' names all the while. But it was hopeless. Nobody answered.

"For all I know," he said to himself, gloomily, "I'm just flying farther away from Brisa and Kona and Sumatra. For all I know, I'm flying *upside down*! Oh, and by the way—I *hate* the dark."

Sirocco shook his head. He was babbling. And he was flying off to who knew where. He was *losing* it!

"Because I'm all alone!" he said, babbling more.

Then suddenly, he heard a voice. But not with his ears. The voice was inside his head.

It was Kona! With a start, Sirocco realized he knew *just* what she'd say if she were there.

"Stop and take a deep breath," she'd tell him in that cool, motherly way of hers. *"Just clear your mind and* calm down."

So Sirocco did. He hovered in the air and breathed in the cool night air.

Sirocco blinked. The deep breath had helped. A little bit, anyway.

"Think of something pretty!"

That was Brisa's voice in his head, now. Sirocco smiled a little and pictured the Wind Dancers' apple tree house covered with juicy red apples.

Finally, he heard the imaginary voice of Sumatra.

"*Look around,*" said the resourceful filly. "*You can see more than you think.*"

At this, Sirocco snorted—but he also followed the filly's advice. He squinted into the blackness.

"Nothing here," he declared. He turned slowly. "And . . . nothing there."

His voice began to shake again as he continued to spin around. "I see nothing, nothing, noth—hey!"

Sirocco gasped.

Because he'd suddenly seen . . . something!

It was a light! And it was (Sirocco was pretty sure) too low and steady to be a star.

"Yaaaaay," Sirocco neighed and began flying as fast as he could toward the comforting glimmer of gold.

In only a minute, he arrived at the light and discovered that it was coming from the front porch of a house! In its glow, he could see that the house was yellow and that it had a screen door and big windows next to it.

Sirocco recognized this place.

"This is Leanna's house!" he cried happily. "Which means I'm still in the dandelion meadow. I thought I'd flown miles away!"

Sirocco darted around to the side of the house and smiled as he peered inside Leanna's open bedroom window. There, he saw a soft glow coming from a night-light, and Leanna fast asleep.

Then, his happiness vanished.

Because Sirocco's friend looked almost as unhappy as he felt—even though she was sleeping. The slumbering girl tossed and turned, and rubbed her closed eyes.

"She must be having a bad dream," Sirocco said to himself. "Too bad she doesn't have a sleep buddy to keep her company."

Jeepers' fuzzy face appeared in Sirocco's mind.

"I know just how that feels," he added with a sigh.

After a few minutes of gazing at Leanna, Sirocco cocked his head thoughtfully.

Huh! he realized. *I kind of feel not so awful anymore.*

Maybe it was being near Leanna that had comforted him.

Or maybe it was imagining his buddy Jeepers.

Or maybe, Sirocco thought, turning to gaze out at the dark dandelion meadow, *it's knowing that I'm not really all alone. Kona, Sumatra, and Brisa are out there. Waiting for me.*

Sirocco straightened up suddenly.

And not just waiting. They're probably worrying, too! Unlike me, I bet they're still lost in the dark.

Sirocco pictured them.

Sumatra, who liked everything neat and tidy, surely hated not knowing where she was.

And Kona was probably struggling to comfort everyone, despite her jitters.

And what about Brisa? Sirocco wondered. *In the dark, she can't look at her pretty magic jewels or her long blond mane. Brisa without her beauty? She'll go crazy!*

Sirocco reared back on his hind legs and kicked at the air with his forelegs. Once again, he'd shaken off his shivers and forgotten his night fright.

"My friends need me!" he whinnied.

Sirocco pictured himself flying to the fillies' rescue.

He imagined them crying with relief as he guided them back to the safety of Leanna's night-light.

And then, he imagined Sumatra saying, *"Sirocco, I never knew you could be so brave!"*

Sirocco grinned.

"Forget being a scaredy-horse," he declared triumphantly. "I'm going to be a *hero*!"

Then, he dashed from the comforting glow of Leanna's bedroom window—and was quickly swallowed back up by the dark!

CHAPTER 6

A Bump in the Night

The only glitch in Sirocco's plan to rescue his scared friends was this: They weren't so scared.

In fact, while Sirocco was dashing to the fillies' "rescue," Sumatra, Kona, and Brisa were passing their time in the dark giggling and telling stories!

"So, then," Sumatra said, grinning into the darkness and stroking her ribbon blanket as she finished a funny tale she'd been telling Kona and Brisa, "I said to the bee, 'Hey, I don't even know you. And you call me *honey*?'"

Kona burst out laughing in great, wheezy neighs, while Brisa giggled with staccato whinnies.

"Sumatra," Brisa said, "you should really take your show on the road! Don't you think, Siroc— Oh! I almost forgot. Sirocco isn't here with us."

"I sure hope he's okay," Kona said, her

laughter dying quickly. "I don't think this adventure is turning out the way he expected."

"Please," Sumatra scoffed. "If I know him, he's flown up above the clouds to zip around in the moonlight."

"Ooh, I don't think so," Brisa said. Her voice sounded as concerned as Kona's now. "We all know that Sirocco's been acting sort of funny tonight."

"Yes, and not funny as in ha-ha," Kona noted. "But funny as in scared—*OW!*"

Kona had been interrupted by something that hit her with a giant *whomp!*

And at exactly the same time as the *whomp,* the cloud that had been covering up the moon (or the moon that had been hiding behind the cloud, depending on which Wind Dancer you agree with) shifted. Sumatra and Brisa blinked in the sudden burst of moonlight. Kona was nowhere to be seen!

But in her place was—

"*Sirocco!*" Brisa burst out. "You're back!"

"I'm back!" Sirocco replied, looking around blearily. He seemed just as surprised as Brisa. "But where's Kona?"

The leaves of a nearby maple tree rustled.

"Over here," came Kona's muffled voice.

A moment later, the violet filly emerged from the tree, looking a little woozy but uninjured. She grinned at Sirocco. "I know you wanted some sweet shoofly pie, but tossing me hard enough to knock maple syrup out of that tree is going a little too far, don't you think?"

"Sorry," Sirocco muttered. "That wasn't part of my plan."

"So, where *were* you all this time?" Kona asked him as she rejoined the group.

"Were you lost in the dark?" Brisa asked Sirocco sympathetically.

"And scared witless?" Sumatra added kindly.

"Lost?" Sirocco cried indignantly. "Scared? No, I was flying around looking for you guys!"

Sirocco's eyes looked shifty.

"You know," he added, "to rescue you!"

Then he puffed out his chest a bit.

"And I was definitely NOT scared," he continued.

"Oh, no?" Sumatra said skeptically.

"No way!" Sirocco said with a grin. He held out his front hooves to the fillies. "You girls are sure lucky I kept my cool in the dark."

While Sumatra stifled a snort, Kona and Brisa exchanged a playful look.

"Speaking of keeping cool in the dark," Kona said to the colt, "I bet there are a lot more things you'd like to do before the sun comes up, huh? You know, like explore the *darkest* corners of the barn at Leanna's farm."

Sirocco looked a little uncomfortable.

"Or go for a midnight swim in the pond," Brisa suggested with a glint in her eye. "You know, the deep one in the middle of the woods."

Now, the colt squirmed.

"Or," Sumatra added with her own grin,

"we could go dig in that big hollow log near our apple tree. It'd be real fun in the dark, don't you think?"

"No, *no*, and NO!" Sirocco burst out.

When the fillies looked at him in mock surprise, Sirocco quickly added, "I mean . . . that's a nice offer and all. But I dragged you out of your sleeping stalls for this. I'd understand if you wanted to go home, to our nice, warm, *cozy* stalls instead."

The fillies exchanged one more secret smile. Then Sumatra stretched and yawned loudly.

"You know," she sighed, "I *am* actually pretty tired."

"And I didn't realize I'm hungry," Brisa said.

"And carrying Charles around all night has made my neck sore," Kona added, glancing over her shoulder at her teddy bear.

Then she cocked her head and looked at Sirocco.

"I don't suppose you'd carry Charles home for me, would you?" she asked.

Kona turned her head and nipped her teddy bear out from under her flower necklace.

Sirocco didn't hesitate. He grabbed the teddy bear with his teeth, then placed Charles

between his front hooves.

As Sirocco gazed down at Charles, he didn't notice Kona, Sumatra, and Brisa exchanging one more playful grin.

"So home, then?" Kona said soothingly. "Maybe we can even make you shoofly pie when we get there."

This time, it was Sirocco who answered with a glint in his eye.

"Oh, I don't know," he said, noticing that the sky started turning toward dawn. "I've suddenly got a second wind. Care to go on one more adventure?"

The three fillies gaped at the colt.

"Sirocco, you *can't* be serious?" Kona said.

In response, Sirocco burst out laughing. And he laughed—loudly and confidently—the rest of the way home.

Good Night, Sleep Tight!

You'd think after their all-nighter, the Wind Dancers would have stayed home the *next* night.

But instead, at bedtime, they were once again flying across the dark dandelion meadow.

Back to Leanna's house.

The four Wind Dancers fluttered to their friend's bedroom window and landed on the windowsill. They peeked in. Once again, Leanna was tossing and turning in her sleep.

"See," Sirocco said to the fillies. "It's like I told you—Leanna could really use a sleep buddy."

With a grin, Sirocco turned his head and peeked at the fuzzy green and orange frog perched on his back.

"Isn't that right, Jeepers?"

"Brisina certainly agrees," Brisa said, gazing fondly at the toy horse dangling from her magic jewel.

"So does Charles," Kona said, giving her own sleep buddy a nose nuzzle.

"So do I," Sumatra added, snuggling under her ribbon-y blanket buddy.

The Wind Dancers returned their gazes to Leanna, and then Sirocco looked downward. Tucked between his forelegs was one more sleep buddy.

It was a fuzzy, winged horse.

The toy horse was made of Wind Dancer magic. Its reins were crafted from Sumatra's magical ribbons, and it wore a necklace of Brisa's sparkly jewels. The horse also had a mane made of Kona's magic flowers, and a tail just like Sirocco's beautiful butterflies.

Sirocco landed on the edge of Leanna's bed and tiptoed across her pillow. Then, ever so gently, he slipped the soft toy next to her.

Holding his breath, Sirocco flew back to his friends on the windowsill.

"Look!" Sumatra noted. "It's working already!"

It was true. Leanna's furrowed forehead had smoothed out. And now, she was sleeping with her arms around her own little Wind

Dancer sleep buddy.

Sirocco grinned at his friends.

"And now . . ." he said excitedly.

"Shh!" the fillies all said together. Even though they knew they were invisible to Leanna, they wanted to be sure they didn't wake her.

". . . let's go hit the hay, too!" Sirocco finished, changing his voice to a whisper.

Here's a sneak preview of *Wind Dancers* Book 5:

Heads Up, Horses!

CHAPTER 1
Kick Off!

It was a bright day in the dandelion meadow, but Kona's mood wasn't nearly as sunny as the weather. In fact, as the Wind Dancers flew over the field of dandelions, soaking up the first minutes of morning, she was feeling as blue as the sky.

"I don't know *what* we should do today," she sighed, flying over to a branch of a big oak tree and kicking an acorn. It sailed through the air and landed with a neat *plunk* in an abandoned bird's nest in a neighboring tree.

"Looks to me like you're doing *something* already!" Sumatra said, impressed.

"What do you mean?" Kona asked.

"Hello? You just made a nest-in-one!" Sirocco pointed out. He kicked at the air, only to send himself into a wobbly double backflip. "*Whoa!*"

"As you can see," Sumatra said dryly as the Wind Dancers flew on, "not everyone has your kicking talent, Kona."

"That's why you were such a star in Sumatra's talent show!" Brisa added sweetly.

"That's nice of you to say," Kona said, sighing again, "but lately—what can I say?—my kicking has kind of . . . lost its kick for me."

The horses had arrived over the tall, wooden fence that surrounded the elementary school. Idly, Kona reached out and tapped her front hoof against a pinecone dangling from a nearby tree branch. The cone landed in a knot in the fence and stuck fast!

Sirocco gaped at Kona's bull's-eye.

"You're such a kicker!" he sputtered.

Kona tried to smile at Sirocco, but she feared it came out as more of a frown.

"Here's the thing," Kona said to her friends. "Sumatra's talent show is *so* last month. Now, I've got nobody to entertain with my kicking."

"That doesn't mean you have to stop practicing," Sumatra encouraged Kona. "With every kick, you're getting better and better at hitting targets!"

"But I think I've kicked every acorn, rock, and apple in this meadow," Kona answered. She swooped down and kicked up a pebble on the ground with her front hoof. Then she rose back into the air, casually juggling the stone from hoof to hoof. "And I've kicked them at every tree knot, branch, and bird's nest I could possibly find."

· · ·

"Over here! Kick it!"

"Who said that?" Kona exclaimed. She was so stunned, she fumbled her pebble and dropped it!

Continue the magical adventures with Breyer's

Wind Dancers

Let your imagination fly!

Sumatra

Sirocco

Kona

Brisa

BREYER®

Collect them all!

For horse fun that never ends!